Sam and Jack

Three Stories

Sam and Jack
Three Stories

Alex Moran

Illustrated by Tim Bowers

Green Light Readers
Harcourt, Inc.
San Diego   New York   London

Requests for permission to make copies of any part of the work should be mailed to the following address: Permissions Department, Harcourt, Inc., 6277 Sea Harbor Drive, Orlando, Florida 32887-6777.

www.harcourt.com

First Green Light Readers edition 2001
Green Light Readers is a trademark of Harcourt, Inc., registered in the United States of America and/or other jurisdictions.

Library of Congress Cataloging-in-Publication Data
Moran, Alex.
Sam and Jack/Alex Moran; illustrated by Tim Bowers.
p. cm.
"Green Light Readers."
Summary: Sam the mouse and Jack the cat overcome their differences and become friends.
[1. Cats—Fiction. 2. Mice—Fiction. 3. Friendship—Fiction.]
I. Bowers, Tim, ill. II. Title.
PZ7.M788193Sam 2001
[E]—dc21   2001000413
ISBN 0-15-216240-2
ISBN 0-15-216234-8 (pb)

A C E G H F D B
A C E G H F D B (pb)

A Surprise

I see a mat.

I see a hat on a mat.

I see a tail on a mat.

I see a cat on a mat.

It is Jack the cat!

Jack

Are you a cat?

I am a cat.

Are you a friend?

I am a friend.

I am your funny friend, Jack.

Sam

I am Sam.

I am little.

I am big.

I am sad.

I am happy.

Meet the Illustrator

Tim Bowers loves to draw pictures of animals. Dogs were his favorite animal to paint when he was a young boy. He painted many pictures of his own dog, which still hang in his parents' house today! Now he enjoys drawing all sorts of different animals.